My Alphabet Safari

By Evelynn Ogwang

CW00867663

AuthorHouse™
1663 Liberty Drive
Bloomington, IN 47403
www.authorhouse.com
Phone: 1-800-839-8640

© 2012 Evelynn Ogwang. All rights reserved.

No part of this book may be reproduced, stored in a retrieval system,
or transmitted by any means without the written permission of the author.

First published by AuthorHouse 01/26/2012

ISBN: 978-1-4567-5621-5 (sc)

Library of Congress Control Number: 2011904890

Printed in the United States of America

Any people depicted in stock imagery provided by Thinkstock are models,
and such images are being used for illustrative purposes only.

Certain stock imagery © Thinkstock.

This book is printed on acid-free paper.

Because of the dynamic nature of the Internet, any web addresses or links contained in this book may have changed
since publication and may no longer be valid. The views expressed in this work are solely those of the author and do not
necessarily reflect the views of the publisher, and the publisher hereby disclaims any responsibility for them.

authorHOUSE®

Dedication

To Azenath & Elisha Ogwang, Helena Nyangoje, Maria Awino, Rona Pearce, Harry & Josie Beylerian, Ngasseu, Alvin, Alexis &Julius

To my wonderful family and friends

My Alphabet Safari

Aa Bb Cc

Gg Hh Ii Jj

Nn Oo Pp

Uu Vv Ww

Dd   Ee   Ff

Kk   Ll   Mm

Qq   Rr   Ss   Tt

Xx   Yy   Zz

Aa

Aardvark

Aardvarks are also called ant bears. They have a long tongue for eating termites.

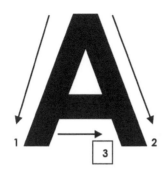 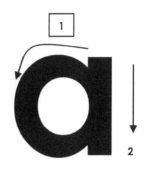

Trace over the letters below using your finger.
Follow the arrows in the example above.

A A A

a a a a

Bb

Buffalo

Buffaloes eat more at night than during the day.

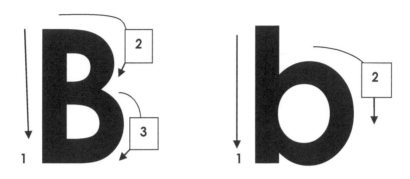

Trace over the letters below using your finger.
Follow the arrows in the example above.

B B B B B

b b b b

Cheetah

Cheetahs are the world's fastest land mammals. Cheetahs can go from zero to sixty miles (ninety six kilometres) an hour in three seconds.

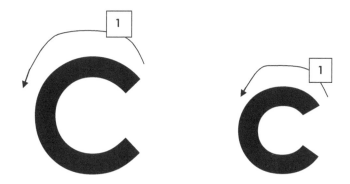

Trace over the letters below using your finger.
Follow the arrows in the example above.

Dd

Dikdik

Dikdiks produce whistling sounds through their noses when frightened.

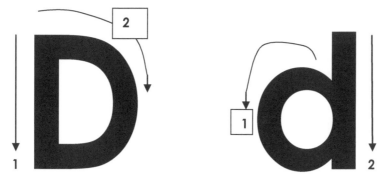

Trace over the letters below using your finger.
Follow the arrows in the example above.

DDDD

dddd

Ee

Elephant

Elephants are the largest land animals on earth.

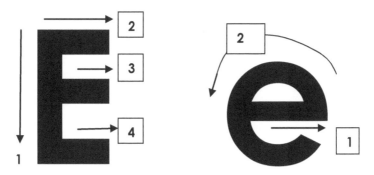

Trace over the letters below using your finger.
Follow the arrows in the example above.

EEEEE

eeee

Ff

Flamingo

Flamingos have filter like structures in their beaks to remove food from muddy water before they expel the liquid.

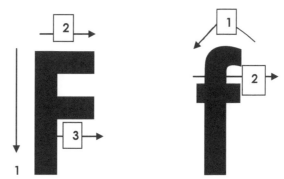

Trace over the letters below using your finger.
Follow the arrows in the example above.

F F F F F F

f f f f f f f f

Gg

Giraffe

Giraffes are the tallest living animals. Giraffes and human beings both have seven vertebrae in their necks.

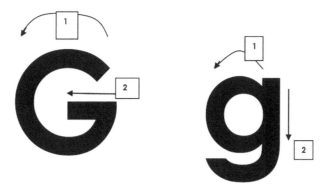

Trace over the letters below using your finger.
Follow the arrows in the example above.

G G G

g g g g

Hh

Hippo

Hippos are also called hippopotamuses.
Hippos are good swimmers and can hold their
breath under water for up to five minutes.

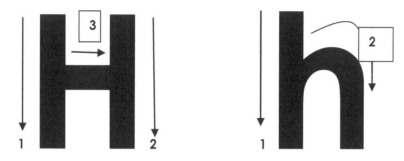

Trace over the letters below using your finger.
Follow the arrows in the example above.

HHHHH

hhhhh

Impala

Impalas can leap distances up to thirty-three feet (ten meters). A running impala will jump over anything in its path.

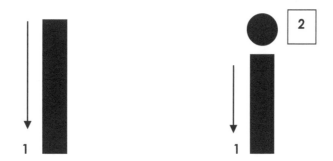

Trace over the letters below using your finger.
Follow the arrows in the example above.

23

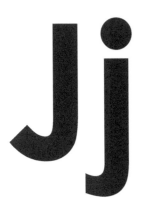

Jj

Jackal

Jackals have doglike features and bushy tails.

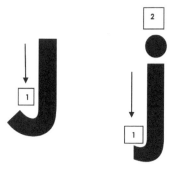

Trace over the letters below using your finger.
Follow the arrows in the example above.

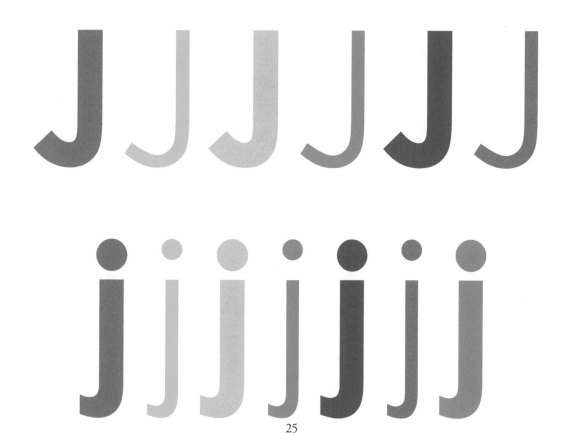

Kk

Kudu

Kudus have stripes and spots on their body. Their horns can grow as long as seventy-two inches and make two and a half graceful twists.

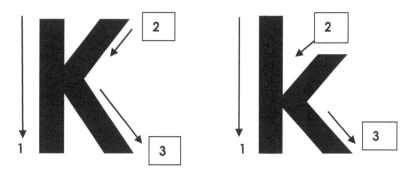

Trace over the letters below using your finger.
Follow the arrows in the example above.

K K K K K

k k k k k

Ll

Lion

Lions are the only cats that live in groups.
These groups are called prides.

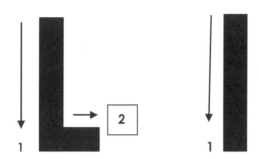

Trace over the letters below using your finger.
Follow the arrows in the example above.

Mm

Meerkat

Meerkats are also called suricates. They are mongooses. They are often in an upright posture by standing on their rear legs.

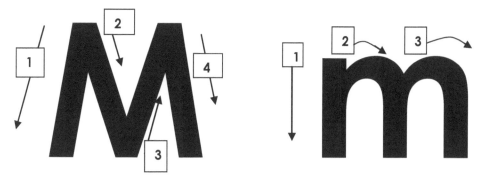

Trace over the letters below using your finger.
Follow the arrows in the example above.

Nn

Nudibranch

Nudibranchs are sea slugs. They have the most fascinating shapes, colours and patterns of any animal on earth.

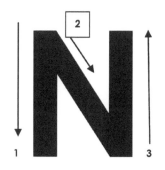 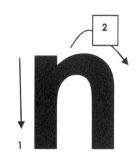

Trace over the letters below using your finger.
Follow the arrows in the example above.

N N N N

n n n n n

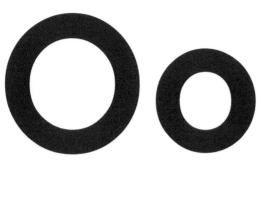

Ostrich

Ostriches are the world's largest birds.

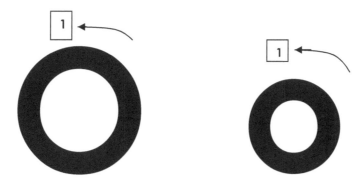

Trace over the letters below using your finger.
Follow the arrows in the example above.

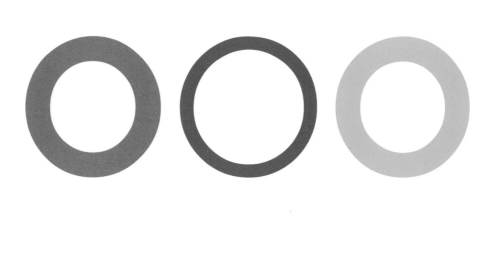

Pp

Peacock

Peacocks are male peafowl. Females
are called peahens.

Trace over the letters below using your finger.
Follow the arrows in the example above.

PPPPP

pppp

Qq

Quail

Quails are usually seen in groups called coveys.

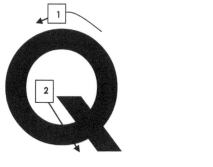

Trace over the letters below using your finger.
Follow the arrows in the example above.

Q Q Q

q q q q

Rr

Rhino

Rhinos are also called rhinoceros. Black rhinos eat from trees and bushes. White rhinos graze on grasses.

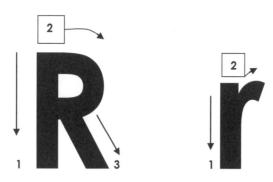

Trace over the letters below using your finger.
Follow the arrows in the example above.

RRRRR

rrrrrrrrr

Ss

Secretary bird

Secretary birds have eagle-like bodies on crane-like legs.

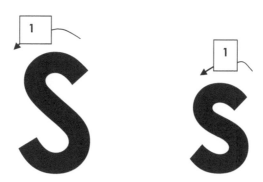

Trace over the letters below using your finger.
Follow the arrows in the example above.

SSSSS

SSSSSS

Tt

Tortoise

Tortoises graze on leaves, grass and cactus. Giant tortoises can reach five hundred and fifty pounds (over two hundred and fifty kilograms) and some can exceed five feet (one and a half meters) in length.

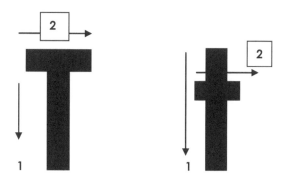

Trace over the letters below using your finger.
Follow the arrows in the example above.

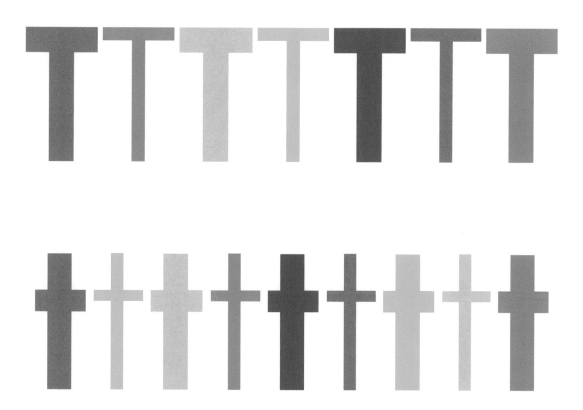

U u

Umbretta

The umbretta is also known as the hammer-head.

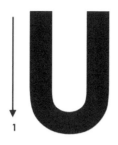 

Trace over the letters below using your finger.
Follow the arrows in the example above.

U U U U

U U U U U

Vv

Vervet monkey

Vervet monkeys are good climbers, jumpers and swimmers.

Trace over the letters below using your finger.
Follow the arrows in the example above.

Ww

Warthog

Warthogs have four sharp tusks. They use empty dens created by aardvarks as hidey-holes.

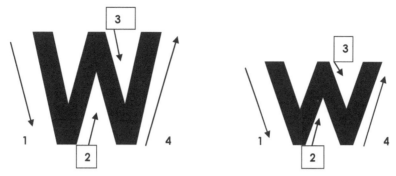

Trace over the letters below using your finger.
Follow the arrows in the example above.

X is found in e**X**tinct. The quagga is an extinct
zebra-like animal that lived in southern Africa.

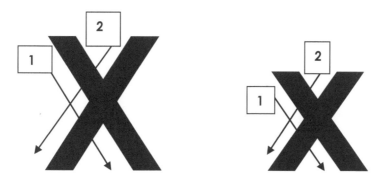

Trace over the letters below using your finger.
Follow the arrows in the example above.

Yy

Yellow weaver bird

Yellow weaver birds make the most elaborately woven nests of birds.

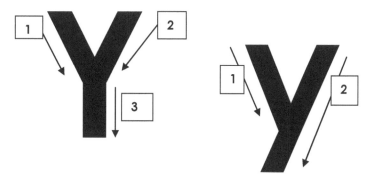

Trace over the letters below using your finger.
Follow the arrows in the example above.

Y Y Y Y Y

y y y y y

Zz

Zebra

Zebra stripe patterns are as distinctive
as fingerprints in human beings.

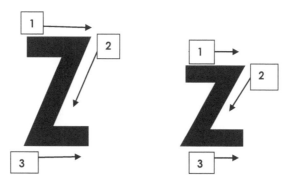

Trace over the letters below using your finger.
Follow the arrows in the example above.

ZZZZZZ

ZZZZZZ

Lightning Source UK Ltd.
Milton Keynes UK
UKHW051930091222
413694UK00002B/42